CHERISHED FAIRY TALES

Pinocchio

illustrated by Jim Talbot
retold by Dandi

In a mountain village in Italy, lived a poor carpenter named Gepetto. The old man carved cuckoo clocks, wind-up toys, rocking horses – all of wood.

Yet even surrounded by such wondrous toys, Gepetto was lonely. He longed for a son.

One day Gepetto received an unusual piece of wood from his aged teacher, Master Cherry. "I will make the finest puppet and call him Pinocchio," vowed Gepetto.

In the corner of the shop, an enchanted Cricket looked on as Gepetto carved the wooden boy. The wood seemed to move in his hands. "If only you *could* move," Gepetto muttered, painting the final eyebrow.

That night as Gepetto slept, Pinocchio began to move. He raised his elbows with no strings attached! He opened his wooden jaw, bent his knees, then jumped. "Papa!" he shouted.

Gepetto came running. "My wish has come true!" he cried.

They danced until dawn. Even the Cricket joined in.

Gepetto rose early, put on his only costly possession, his wool coat, and dashed to town. When he returned, the old man, now coatless, presented Pinocchio with a stack of books. "All good boys must go to school," he said.

"Where is your coat?" asked Pinocchio.

"School is more important than a coat," Gepetto answered.

Pinocchio knew his Papa had sold his coat to buy the books. "My wonderful Papa!" he cried.

Pinocchio skipped down the cobblestone until he tripped. He looked up into the face of a Fox.

"Where are you headed in such haste?" crooned the Fox.

"I'm on my way to school," said Pinocchio.

"You don't want to go to school!" returned the Fox. "Come with me to the Puppet Theater."

"Don't listen to him," warned the enchanted Cricket.

But the Theater sounded like much more fun than school. So Pinocchio followed the sly Fox.

"You can't see the show for free!" bellowed Fire Eater, the puppet showman.

Pinocchio stared at Fire Eater's ink black beard that reached to the ground. "I have no money," he said weakly.

"Sell your books to me for the price of a ticket," suggested Fox, knowing he could resell them for profit.

So Pinocchio sold his books, feeling a pang of guilt as he remembered Gepetto shivering at home.

Pinocchio was so caught up with the Puppet Show, he leaped on stage. The other puppets stopped their dancing.

Fire Eater stormed the stage, grabbed Pinocchio, and hung him from a nail by his shirt collar. "That will teach you to ruin my show!" he roared.

Pinocchio began to sob. "My poor Papa." And he poured out his heart to the Fire Eater, whose own frozen heart began to thaw.

"Poor Gepetto," said the Fire Eater at last. He set Pinocchio down and gave him five gold coins. "Go home, obey your Papa, and go to school."

"Now we can go home," whispered Cricket.

With his gold coins clinking in his pocket,
Pinocchio headed home. "I will buy my Papa a golden
coat with diamond buttons!" he told Cricket.

"You can't go home!" said Fox, his cane hooked
on Pinocchio's arm. "Come to Donkey Island, where
you can turn your five gold coins into 2,000 overnight!
Plant them in the magic ground, and by morning you'll
be rich!"

"Don't do it, Pinocchio," begged Cricket.

But with more promises from Fox, Pinocchio
sailed for Donkey Island.

"You can do as you like here," said Fox, as he watched Pinocchio bury the five gold coins.

Later, Pinocchio downed candy and lollipops. On greasy French fries, he shook salt and pepper from shakers shaped like donkeys.

Then he noticed an amazing thing. The children on the Island had sprouted long ears and a tail! Pinocchio's own hat popped up. Donkey Island was turning them into donkeys!

"I want my coins back!" cried Pinocchio. "I want to go home!"

But he was too late. Fox had dug up the coins for himself.

Just then, Cricket appeared. "Where are your coins?" he asked.

Pinocchio felt ashamed and didn't want Cricket to think him a donkey. "I lost my coins." He felt something move on his face, but he went on lying. "I was almost home when a dragon captured me and flew me here against my will!"

Pinocchio glanced down and saw his own nose, growing longer with every lie!

"Yes, Pinocchio," said the Cricket. "When you lie, it's as plain as the nose on your face."

"I'm sorry I lied," cried Pinocchio.

"You must be brave and true," said Cricket. "I have bad news. Your Papa, who has searched for you since you left home, has met with an accident and is lost at sea."

"Papa!" Determined to save his Papa, Pinocchio dove off Donkey Island, the Fox close at his heels.

Pinocchio swam for hours until he spotted his
Papa's boat sticking out of the mouth of a giant fish.

Bravely the little puppet swam to the open mouth.
Down the giant throat he slid, down, down – right into
the arms of Gepetto.

"My boy!" cried Gepetto.

"Follow me, Papa. I'll save you."

Pinocchio pulled the donkey pepper shaker from his pocket and shook it all out on the fish's tongue. He grabbed Gepetto's hand and waited.

"AA-A-A-CHOO!" The fish spew out Pinocchio and his Papa, right at the feet of the Cricket! But the enchanted Cricket had turned into a beautiful Blue-haired Fairy.

"You saved me!" cheered Gepetto.

But Pinocchio was lying face down in the sand.

Sadly, the old woodcarver picked up his son.
"Oh, my brave and true boy!"

"Pinocchio," called the Fairy. "Because you were
unselfish and true, you have earned the right to become
a real, live boy." And she kissed the wooden puppet.

Pinocchio's nose began to shrink. His donkey ears and tail disappeared. He blinked his eyes open and jumped up.

"Papa!" he cried. "I'm a real, live boy!"

Gepetto and Pinocchio lived happily ever after. Pinocchio went to school and learned to make wooden puppets of his own. But he always made them with little, tiny noses...just in case.